DATE DUE

JUL 6 1993		
AUG 2 3 1993		
DEC 0 2 1993		
NOV 0 2 1995		
APR 23 '03		
MAY 6 2006		

Demco, Inc. 38-293

A NOTE TO PARENTS

When your children are ready to "step into reading," giving them the right books—and lots of them—is as crucial as giving them the right food to eat. **Step into Reading Books** present exciting stories and information reinforced with lively, colorful illustrations that make learning to read fun, satisfying, and worthwhile. They are priced so that acquiring an entire library of them is affordable. And they are beginning readers with an important difference—they're written on four levels.

Step 1 Books, with their very large type and extremely simple vocabulary, have been created for the very youngest readers. **Step 2 Books** are both longer and slightly more difficult. **Step 3 Books,** written to mid-second-grade reading levels, are for the child who has acquired even greater reading skills. **Step 4 Books** offer exciting nonfiction for the increasingly proficient reader.

Children develop at different ages. **Step into Reading Books,** with their four levels of reading, are designed to help children become good—and interested—readers *faster*. The grade levels assigned to the four steps—preschool through grade 1 for Step 1, grades 1 through 3 for Step 2, grades 2 and 3 for Step 3, and grades 2 through 4 for Step 4—are intended only as guides. Some children move through all four steps very rapidly; others climb the steps over a period of several years. These books will help your child "step into reading" in style!

J
Fic
Bru

Library of Congress Cataloging-in-Publication Data: Brunhoff, Laurent de. Babar's little circus star. (Step into reading. A Step 1 book) SUMMARY: Unhappy because she is the smallest in the family, Isabelle discovers that being little has its advantages when she is asked to perform in the circus. [1. Elephants—Fiction.   2. Circus—Fiction.   3. Size—Fiction] I. Title.   II. Series: Step into reading. Step 1 book.   PZ7.B82843Babm   1988   [E]   87-14149 ISBN: 0-394-88959-2 (pbk.); 0-394-98959-7 (lib. bdg.)

Manufactured in the United States of America

STEP INTO READING is a trademark of Random House, Inc.

0

Step into Reading

BABAR'S
Little Circus Star

By Laurent de Brunhoff

A Step 1 Book

Random House 🏠 New York

4

Isabelle is the baby
of the family.
Everybody loves her—
Babar most of all.

But Isabelle does not like
being so little.
She cannot climb trees
like the other children.

She cannot ride
a big bike.
"Wait for me!"
cries Isabelle.

CELESTEVILLE SCHOOL DISTRICT

She is too little
to go to school.

And she has to go to bed
before everybody else.

"I hate being little!"
Isabelle cries.
Her mother tells her,
"Sometimes it is nice
to be little.

"I always give you
the rose on the cake.

And no one else
can sit on top of Papa."

Isabelle knows that.
But she is still sad.

Today the children
are very excited.
The circus is in town.

"I am going to be
a circus star one day!"
says Isabelle.
The children just laugh.

Then Isabelle does
a flip,

a split,

and a handstand.

The clowns watch her.

"We need a little clown,"
   they say.

"You are very good,
   and you are just the right size.

Can you come with us?"

Isabelle asks Mama and Papa.

They say yes.

Isabelle and the clown

go off to the circus.

Isabelle is so happy.

"I am going to be

a circus star!"

The clowns show Isabelle
what to do.

The show is about
to begin!

Out come the clowns.

"Look!
There is Isabelle!"
shouts Babar.

Isabelle comes out again.
She is ready
for her next trick.

She sits down
on one end
of a seesaw.
What will happen next?

A big hippo jumps on
the other side.

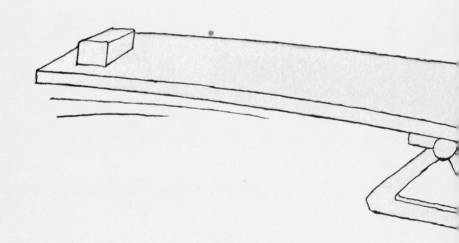

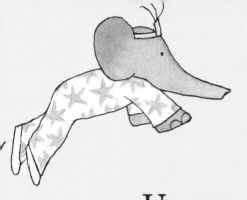

Up, up, up
goes Isabelle.

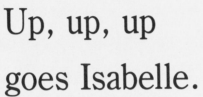

And she lands
in a little chair!

Everyone claps.
"Hooray for Isabelle!"
they shout.

After the show
Isabelle goes home
with her family.

"I am tired,"
she says.

Babar picks her up.

Sometimes it is nice
to be little!